Squishy McFluff
The Invisible Cat

Meets Mad
Nana Dot

For beautiful Ruby.
Also for Ava and my brilliantly bonkers Mum,
the inspiration behind Mad Nana XXX

First published in the UK in 2015
First published in the US in 2018
by Faber and Faber Limited
Bloomsbury House
74–77 Great Russell Street
London WC1B 3DA

Designed by Faber and Faber
Printed in Malta

The right of Pip Jones and Ella Okstad to be identified as author
and illustrator of this work respectively has been asserted in
accordance with Section 77 of the
Copyright, Designs and Patents Act 1988

ISBN 978–0571–30254–3

4 6 8 10 9 7 5 3

Squishy McFluff
The Invisible Cat

Meets
Mad Nana Dot

by *Pip Jones*

Illustrated by *Ella Okstad*

x

FABER & FABER

Can you see him? My kitten?

His tiny pink nose?

He's ever so nimble

And quick on his toes!

Imagine him, quick!

Have you imagined enough?

Oh, good! You can see him!

It's Squishy McFluff!

All through the summer time

Ava had played,

Tumbling through sunshine,

bumbling in shade,

Jumping and skipping –

the games had no end

With Squishy McFluff,

her invisible friend!

They dressed up as pirates,

and dressed up as kings,

And flew like the birds

(with some help

from the swings).

Squishy and Ava climbed trees!

And picked flowers!

And used Mummy's plant pots

to make wobbly towers!

They sculpted a mud chute

to slide on their bellies,

Built houses for hedgehogs

using Dad's wellies.

They found a big hose!

And they had SO much fun

Making fountains to jump through

in the hot sun.

(They also discovered,

   if they closed the door tight,

The shed filled RIGHT up

   if they left it all night!)

So with mud on his paws

and mud on her knees,

They were happy as bunnies

and busy as bees –

But while Squishy McFluff

had kept Ava spellbound,

She'd not really noticed

her Mum get so round . . .

Well, sunset one evening,

when the sky was aglow,

Dad's voice shook as he shouted:

'QUICK! TIME TO GO!'

'Now hurry up, Ava,

we really must rush!

'Pack your nightie, your flannel,

Your yellow toothbrush!'

Ava took AGES!

Dad was pacing the hall.

'What are you DOING up there?'

Daddy called.

'I can't find McFluff!'

Ava yelled down the stairs,

'He snuck off and hid

while I packed all my bears!'

14

'We really must GO,' Dad said.

'Don't muck about.

'Wherever he's hiding,

McFluff MUST come out!'

'But I REALLY can't see him!'

Ava replied.

'Of course you can't SEE him!'

poor Daddy cried.

15

'He'll come out RIGHT now,

or he'll have to stay here.'

Well, that was enough

to make Squish

'reappear'!

In the car, on the journey,

Daddy said: 'Right!

'Ava, you'll just need

to stay for one night.

'But darling, no matter

how naughty SQUISH is,

'YOU'D better behave!

So . . . help with the dishes.

'Make toast in the morning.

Remember, Nan's old.

'Be polite . . . and **please**

go to bed when you're told!'

'Yes, Daddy!' said Ava,

enjoying the ride,

While Squishy purred (silently)

there by her side.

'Hey, Squish!' Ava whispered.

'Nan's ever so funny,

'She eats her fried eggs

with bananas and honey.

'Nan loves Christmas SO much!

It's really absurd,

'She puts up her tree

on October the third!

'And Squishy, her garden

is super fantastic.

'She's not good with plants,

so the roses are plastic

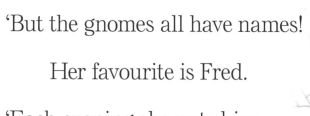

'But the gnomes all have names!

Her favourite is Fred.

'Each evening she puts him

to bed in the shed.

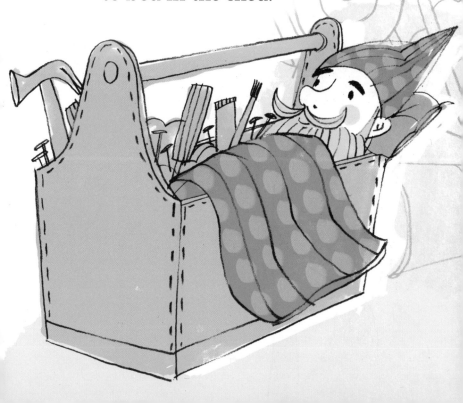

'One time I did hear

my daddy remarking

'That Mad Nana Dot

was "utterly barking."

22

'I'm not sure, perhaps

it's a thing she enjoys

'But I've NEVER heard Nana

make a dog noise . . .'

'We're here!' Daddy said.

'Let's go. Squish as well.'

'Goodie gumdrops!' cried Ava,

'Can we ring the bell?'

'A whole night at Nana's,

just me and my pet.

'I've not even told Nan

about Squishy yet!'

Nana's house, from the outside,

was pleasantly white,

With a flowery front garden –

a calm, tranquil sight.

But inside . . . oh, crumpets!

Squishy's eyes tied in knots!

Each wall, rug and curtain

was covered in spots!

The kettle! The toaster!

    Each pattern the same.

It was obvious how Nana

    got her nickname!

While Dad, rushing off,

    thanked Nan for her troubles,

McFluff bounced around,

    as if catching bubbles.

'Oh Squish!' Ava laughed

(as his backflip went flop).

'They might look like bubbles,

but they really won't pop!'

Nana Dot heard her,

and said: 'Ava, dear!

'I've mislaid my glasses,

is someone else here?'

And then Ava realised

(a little delighted),

Without specs on her nose,

Nan was **very** short-sighted.

'My cat!' Ava told her, 'Look,

Squishy's right there!'

Nan stooped and squinted,

then said (to thin air):

'Aaah! Come to Nana!

Come here little kitty!

'Oh gosh, aren't you sweet?

You're ever so pretty!'

'I'll get you both something,

then bed for you two.

'We'll be busy tomorrow.

I have lots to do!'

Ava guzzled her juice,

but McFluff couldn't drink

A **real** saucer of milk . . .

so it went down the sink.

They both brushed their teeth

and gave Nana a hug.

Then Nan tucked them in,

so they'd sleep nice and snug.

When Ava woke up, Nana said:

'Enough yawning!

'I have a hairdresser's

appointment this morning.'

In the salon, Nan said

to the ladies who sat

Reading and gossiping:

'Don't mind the cat!'

Well, it all seemed as dull

    as the curly-edged pages

Of the hair magazines,

    which had been there for ages.

But McFluff had a thought!

    On the shelf there were lots

Of hair dyes and potions

    in bottles and pots.

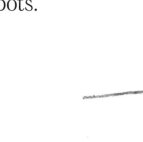

With nobody watching,

and left to their tricks,

Ava grabbed a big bowl

and they started to mix.

'A dollop of this! Ooh,

a big squirt of that!'

How Ava loved

having fun with her cat!

But THEN (eek!) the hairdresser,

terribly busy

Trying his best to make

Nan's hair less frizzy,

Reached for some dye

but took THEIR bowl instead,

And he slopped the strange mixture

all over Nan's head.

It happened so fast!

No time to confess!

The colour they'd made,

it was anyone's guess.

McFluff's legs went weak,

his tail drooped between.

When Nan's towel was removed,

her hair was . . .

45

BRIGHT GREEN!

The ladies all GASPED!

The hairdresser screamed

And began saying 'sorry' . . .

but Nana Dot beamed.

She seemed proud as punch

of her vibrant reflection

And said: 'Oh, how lovely!

I think it's **perfection**!'

The hairdresser gawped,

his mouth open wide

(Which was how he remained

while Nan was blow-dried).

And seeing how Nan's hair

had made her SO pleased,

Ava and Squish grabbed

more bottles and squeeeeezed!

'Quick!' Ava whispered.

'If we make something new,

'The next lucky lady

might get green hair too!'

Later on, Nana said:

'Follow me, round this bend!

'I've a letter to post

and a parcel to send.'

How frightfully boring!

As Ava looked glum,

Squish (silently) miaowed

an idea to his chum.

'Yes Squish! Let's play!

It's our favourite game ever!

'You find the BEST places to hide,

you're so clever!'

So, hiding and seeking

and larking about,

Squish jumped in a postbox . . .

then couldn't get out!

That silly kitten! He should

have known better

Than to squeeze through a hole

the size of a letter.

'Please HELP him!' sobbed Ava,

with a tear in her eye.

'He's scared of the dark, Nan!

The dark makes him cry!'

Well, Nan had to beg

and to plead and implore,

'Til a man with a key came

and opened the door.

Then the mischievous cat

(who no one could see)

Fell out in a heap . . .

he was finally free!

'Where's the kitten?' the chap said,

looking confused.

'I was called off my lunch break!

I could have refused . . .'

'He's here somewhere,'

said Nana, looking perplexed.

Then she gave a loud GASP

at what Ava said next . . .

57

'Behind you! Behind you!

    Mind where you stand!

'He's right by your shoe!

    Now he's sniffing your hand!

'He's climbed on your shoulder!

    His tail's in your ear!

'Look harder! Turn quicker!

    No, not THERE . . . he's here!'

He just didn't know

    where to look, the poor man!

'Get off him, you

    cheeky young kitten!' said Nan.

Then waving her handbag

    and swinging her stick

To shoo McFluff off,

    Nana said: 'Squishy, quick!

'Leave the postman alone,

you'll RUIN his clothes!'

But Nan swung too high . . .

and **bopped** the man's nose!

Nan said: 'Good kitty,

    'have you worked up a hunger?

'We'll make a quick stop

    at my local fishmonger.'

So Ava said: 'Nan,

    'I don't mean to be rude

'But Squishy's quite fussy

    when it comes to his food.'

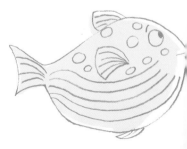

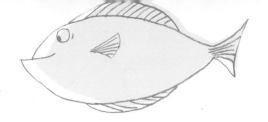

'Yes, I understand,'

Nana said with a nod.

'He surely likes salmon?

Or haddock? Or cod?'

Ava was worried, and

not sure what to do

But Squishy McFluff,

well, that clever cat knew.

63

And, ignoring the look

on the fishmonger's face,

Ava pointed her finger

at a big empty space!

Delighted there wasn't

a charge for the treat,

Nan said: 'Let's go home.

You have someone to meet . . .'

Dad opened the door,

  looking ever so tired.

His eyes grew quite round

  as he grinned and admired

Nana Dot's hair, which he found

  somewhat strange.

'How nice,' Dad said kindly.

  'Green makes a change!

'Now come upstairs Ava,

your mummy's in bed.'

'Is Mum ill?' Ava wondered.

She did as Dad said.

Upstairs, pink-cheeked,

with a much flatter tummy,

Was a loveable, huggable,

kissable Mummy.

Mum squeezed Ava tight

– she had, of course, missed her –

Then said: 'Look, darling,

I made you a SISTER!'

McFluff sniffed the blankets,

and jumped as they wiggled

And Roo, the new baby,

saw Ava and giggled.

Such a sweet, quiet bundle,

surrounded by toys –

But suddenly . . . OH!

WHAT A HORRIBLE NOISE!

Ava shrieked loudly,

while Squish went and hid.

They both watched, astounded

by what Mummy did.

A cuddle! A jiggle!

A rattle! And then . . .

(After slurping and burping)

it was quiet again.

When Dad had explained

that Roo WAS here to stay,

He sent Ava off

with her kitten to play.

They went to the garden,

to fill up the shed.

Then Big Sister Ava

looked thoughtful and said:

'Roo's a **strange** little thing.

She doesn't do talking,

Just giggling and guzzling

and gurgly squawking.

'But what do you think, Squish?

Do we love Baby Roo?'

. . . And Squish (silently) purred

to say 'yes . . . yes, we do'.